Alexander
and the Horse

by Mary Auld and Esther Hernando

W

FRANKLIN WATTS
LONDON•SYDNEY

King Philip was teaching his son,

Prince Alexander, to fight. The king was

the best fighter in all of Greece.

"Use your shield to block me," said the king.

"Now hit me as I fall back."

Just then, a servant came running up.

"My lord," she said. "A man selling horses
is here. He is in the field outside the palace."

"Take your cloak, my son," said the king.

"Let's go and see this horse seller. I think
it is time you had your own horse."

There were about ten horses for sale,
but as soon as Alexander saw them,
he knew which horse he wanted.

It was the huge horse with a white mark between his eyes. The horse looked scared. He reared up and tossed his head.

5

The horse seller stood by the big horse.

"This is my best animal," he said.

"You can buy him for as much silver

as he weighs."

The king told one of his men to ride the horse.

The horse quickly threw the man off.

The king told another of his men to try.

Again, the horse threw the man. A third man

tried, and he also was thrown to the ground.

"I am not going to buy a horse that nobody can ride," said King Philip. Alexander laughed. "The men are bad riders," he said. "I bet I can ride that horse!"

"You are just showing off," said the king. "It could be dangerous and you might get hurt."

"This is the horse I want," said Alexander.
"If I can tame the horse, will you buy him
for me?"
The king agreed. He did not think Alexander
would be able to ride the huge horse.

Slowly, Alexander walked towards the horse.

Everyone else moved away.

Alexander took hold of the horse's bridle.

He whispered softly and gently stroked

the horse's neck. He saw how the horse

tossed his head when he saw his own shadow.

Alexander turned the horse towards the sun. Now the shadow was behind the horse. Alexander also noticed that when his red cloak swished, the horse jumped. "He doesn't like my cloak," said Alexander, and he took it off.

The horse was much calmer now.
Slowly and carefully, Alexander climbed
on his back and gently kicked his sides.
At first, the horse walked, but he soon
got used to having Alexander on his back
and went faster.

The horse felt happy with Alexander.

He seemed to know that Alexander was kind and could be trusted.

Before long, the boy and the horse were galloping around the field. To the people watching, it looked as if they were flying.

Alexander and the horse stopped in front of the king. The crowd cheered as Alexander jumped off the horse.

The horse stood still, even with all the noise. Alexander held his head and stroked his neck. The horse pushed his nose gently into Alexander's hand.

The king was proud. "Well done, my son!"
he cried. "You will have your horse."
The king told his servants to give the seller
as much silver as the horse weighed.

Alexander climbed up onto his horse again and rode slowly back to the palace. The king walked by their side.

"One day, my son," he said, "you will be a great leader. You and your horse will travel far, and you will rule over many people."

The king was right. When Alexander grew up, he had a great army. He led the army into battle riding on his huge horse. Soon he ruled many lands.

He became known as Alexander the Great.

And today, when people remember Alexander, they also remember his huge horse.

Story order

Look at these 5 pictures and captions.
Put the pictures in the right order
to retell the story.

1

Alexander was gentle with the horse.

2

Alexander knew which horse he wanted.

3 The king bought the horse for Alexander.

4 Alexander rode the horse well.

5 The king's men could not ride the horse.

Independent Reading

This series is designed to provide an opportunity for your child to read on their own. These notes are written for you to help your child choose a book and to read it independently.

In school, your child's teacher will often be using reading books which have been banded to support the process of learning to read. Use the book band colour your child is reading in school to help you make a good choice. *Alexander and the Horse* is a good choice for children reading at White Band in their classroom to read independently. The aim of independent reading is to read this book with ease, so that your child enjoys the story and relates it to their own experiences.

About the book

This story is inspired by historical events. Alexander the Great (356-323 BCE) is said to have tamed his horse, Bucephalus. The horse took his master into many battles and became one of the most famous horses in history.

Before reading

Help your child to learn how to make good choices by asking: "Why did you choose this book? Why do you think you will enjoy it?" Ask your child what they know about Alexander the Great. Explain that he became King of Macedonia in 336 BCE, aged 20. In ten years, he created one of the largest empires in history. Look at the cover with your child and ask: "Do you think the boy can ride that horse?" Remind your child that they can break words into groups of syllables or sound out letters to make a word if they get stuck. Decide together whether your child will read the story independently or read it aloud to you.

During reading
Remind your child of what they know and what they can do independently. If reading aloud, support your child if they hesitate or ask for help by telling them the word. If reading to themselves, remind your child that they can come and ask for your help if stuck.

After reading
Support comprehension by asking your child to tell you about the story. Use the story order puzzle to encourage your child to retell the story in the right sequence, in their own words.
The correct sequence can be found on the next page.
Help your child think about the messages in the book that go beyond the story and ask: "How do you think Alexander felt when he was galloping on the horse across the field?"
Give your child a chance to respond to the story: "Did you have a favourite part?"

Extending learning
Help your child predict other possible outcomes of the story by asking: "What do you think would have happened if Alexander had fallen off the horse the first time he rode him? Do you think Alexander would have given up?"
In the classroom, your child's teacher may be teaching comprehension skills, such as how the use of words and phrases can contribute to the meaning. Which words and phrases tell us how Alexander behaved towards the horse? Find examples in the text, such as: 'He whispered softly and gently stroked the horse's neck', 'Slowly and carefully, Alexander climbed on his back and gently kicked his sides'.

Franklin Watts
First published in Great Britain in 2024
by Hodder and Stoughton
Copyright © Hodder and Stoughton, Ltd
Series Editors: Jackie Hamley and Melanie Palmer
Series Advisors and Development Editors: Dr Sue Bodman and Glen Franklin
Series Designers: Cathryn Gilbert and Peter Scoulding

A CIP catalogue record for this book is
available from the British Library.

ISBN 978 1 4451 8910 9 (hbk)
ISBN 978 1 4451 8911 6 (pbk)
ISBN 978 1 4451 9524 7 (ebook)

Printed in China

Franklin Watts
An imprint of
Hachette Children's Group
Part of Hodder and Stoughton
Carmelite House
50 Victoria Embankment
London EC4Y 0DZ

An Hachette UK Company
www.hachette.co.uk

www.reading-champion.co.uk

FSC
www.fsc.org
MIX
Paper | Supporting
responsible forestry
FSC® C104740

Answer to Story order: 2, 5, 1, 4, 3